Two Naughty Angels

Down to Earth

Two Naughty Angels
Down to Earth

Mary Hooper

Illustrated by Lesley Harker

BLOOMSBURY

First published in Great Britain in 1995 by Bloomsbury Publishing Plc
36 Soho Square, London, W1D 3QY

This edition first published in 2008

Text copyright © Mary Hooper 1995
Illustrations copyright © Lesley Harker 1995

The moral rights of the author and illustrator have been asserted

A CIP catalogue record of this book is available from the
British Library

ISBN 978 0 7475 9061 3

All papers used by Bloomsbury Publishing are natural, recyclable products made
from wood grown in well-managed forests. The manufacturing processes conform
to the environmental regulations of the country of origin.

Typeset by Dorchester Typesetting Group Ltd
Printed in Great Britain by Clays Ltd, St Ives Plc

1 3 5 7 9 10 8 6 4 2

www.bloomsbury.com
www.maryhooper.co.uk

Prologue

This story opens in the kind of heaven you might like to imagine: big fluffy clouds, small fluffy clouds and not a lot else besides. Apart from the angels, that is. Our angels are all bright and beautiful – just as angels should be – and they never grow any older. The longer they spend in heaven, though, the mightier grow their wings and the brighter glow their haloes.

They can't remember anything of their lives on earth, their mums or dads, homes or pets, so they never get sad or lonely. What they do get is very slightly bored!

All of them, especially the younger ones, look forward to the treat which comes along every fifty years: a sight of earth through the Archangel's mystical viewing mirror . . .

The Mirror Cracks

Angie stood on the very edge of a cloud looking anxiously around her. Where in heaven had Gaby got to? The Archangel was expecting them to report for their look in the viewing mirror; it would never do to be late.

Without thinking, Angie started to nibble at a fingernail, then checked herself and put her hands behind her back.

Angels *never* had nibbled nails.

There was a *whooshy* noise and a squeal and suddenly Gaby landed on the cloud next to her.

'Oops,' she said. 'Landed a bit short there. I was doing a spot of free-falling.'

'Well, really!' said Angie.

'Have you tried it?'

'Of course not.'

'It's fun. You tuck your wings back and use your nightie as a parachute. It makes a change from –'

'Sssh!' Angie nodded towards a heavenly choir of angels flying past on their way to choral practice. 'Someone will hear you.' She looked at Gaby and frowned. 'Your nightie is all creased. It looks a mess.'

'That's because I was throwing some of the cherubs up in the air and catching them in it,' Gaby said.

Angie tutted. '*Never never let be seen, An angel who's not neat and clean,*' she said. 'I learnt that at Halo Awareness Classes.'

Gaby looked bored. 'Oh, really?'

'You're never going to get a halo,' Angie said, and she pointed to the faint glitter above her own head. 'Look at mine! It's coming along nicely.'

'I can't be bothered with all that,' Gaby said. 'What's the point of classes to teach you to fold your hands tidily and keep your nightie spotless?

4

Anyway, the Archangel's not going to notice the state of my nightie, is he? Old Holy Joe will be too busy practising on that harp of his. Come on, let's go!'

Spreading their wings, they dropped down a couple of clouds to an open area where, as Gaby had predicted, the Archangel was sitting on a large cloud practising his harp solo. He stood up when he saw them, and both angels shrank back a little in awe. He'd been in heaven many hundreds of years, so his wings were large and magnificent, his halo gleaming as bright as gold.

'Ah! Two of the smaller angels from the realms of glory,' he said. 'Gabrielle and Angela, isn't it?'

The two angels nodded shyly.

'How quickly fifty years doth pass! It seemeth only like yesterday you were here for the viewing mirror.' He unrolled a vast scroll. 'Today, when you see again your earthly abode . . .' he began, and then paused, '. . . not your earthly abode as such, of course, for the bricks and mortar where once you resided have long since crumbled away, but the

5

place where you spent your previous life, then perhaps you will take a moment to reflect on the vast . . .'

Gaby yawned: he said this *every* time. As far as she was concerned, the look in the viewing mirror was the only exciting thing that ever happened in heaven. Why didn't he just get on with it?

At last the Archangel turned and brushed a cloud aside and the mirror was revealed. It stood on an easel and was framed in heavy gold; the reflective part was black and mysterious.

'Today we are having a glimpse of something called a *school*,' he said, 'where young ladies such as yourselves learneth about . . .' he paused, looking vague, 'well, about different things.'

He consulted his scroll of parchment. 'We are going to look at Saint Winifred's Convent,' he said, and he stretched out a hand and touched the mirror.

As Gaby and Angie watched, entranced, the mirror's darkness gleamed silver and then gave way to clouds, which gradually parted to reveal a tall, red-brick building some distance away. As they drew closer, they could see girls running about, kicking a ball, playing, talking, laughing.

'Look – girls like us!' Gaby said excitedly.

'But with no wings!' said Angie.

The Archangel smiled kindly. 'Do you desire to view the library, the dining room, the bedrooms or the playground?'

'The dining room!' Angie said.

'No!' Gaby shouted excitedly. 'The playground!'

'Gabrielle! Angels never raiseth their voices,' said

the Archangel mildly.

'Oh, the playground, please!' Gaby pleaded, and she gave the Archangel such a sweet, angelic smile that suddenly the view through the mirror changed and they were able to see the whole playground – and the girls who were playing there – in wonderful close-up.

Gaby and Angie stared wonderingly. It was as if they were in the playground right amongst the girls of Class 1C. They could see exactly what they were wearing (a rather awful yellow and purple uniform) and hear what they were talking about.

'It's as if we're really on earth!' Angie said in amazement.

'We can almost touch them – they're just on the other side of that glass!' said Gaby, putting out her hand to the mirror.

'Do not touch!' warned the Archangel. He could be stern when he had to be.

'They can't see us, can they?' Angie asked.

The Archangel shook his head. 'They can never see us. They sometimes get a glimpse of other, lower angels – those who are on the first or second level. When they see them they call them ghosts.'

'It looks as if it's all right being a girl,' said Gaby rather plaintively. 'They're all *doing* things.' They're not hanging around on clouds all day getting bored, she thought to herself: these girls have fun.

'Their faces are different,' said Angie. 'They haven't all got pretty smiles, long ringlets and pink ribbons!'

'And I think some of them might be quite naughty,' said Gaby gleefully, watching one girl sticking a notice on another's back.

'Observe, if you will, the nearby trees which bloweth in the wind,' said the Archangel. ✱

Just as the Archangel was speaking, something very strange happened: the viewing mirror began to slip sideways on its stand. The stand was made of wood and had been holding the mirror for a thousand years or so, and no one had noticed that

✱ There is no weather in heaven. Every day is just like the last and it's always beautiful and sunny.

9

for the last hundred and four years it had been rotting away.

The Archangel moved forward and tried to steady the mirror, but it was enormously heavy and he couldn't hold it.

As the two small angels watched, open-mouthed, the mirror slid to the floor and cracked from side to side. Suddenly, they could feel a blast of cold air. As well as the girls' voices, they could also hear the school bell ringing and, distantly, the wind rustling through the trees. They could smell something, too: a mixture of trodden grass, earth, dust and school dinners.

'Oh, wow,' said Gaby.

'It's so *real*!' said Angie.

'Stand back! Stand back from the mirror!' commanded the Archangel.

'I don't want to stand back!' cried naughty Gaby, and she measured the distance between the mirror and herself. It looked so exciting out there . . . She made up her mind all at once. 'Are you coming?' she said to Angie.

'C-coming where?' Angie was cowering back, her wings tucked very close to her body.

'Coming with me to earth, of course!' Gaby squealed.

'I couldn't!'

'Yes, you could!' Gaby grasped Angie's hand. 'Come on, let's live a little!'

And before the Archangel could move, Gaby had jumped through the crack in the mirror and was standing in the playground of St Winifred's, with Angie beside her.

2

The Angels Try
to Be Normal

The two angels stared
around
them,
then
at
each
other. Gaby
smiled.

'Hey, Angie, guess what?'
she said.

'Wh-what?'

'Your halo's gone!'

Angie burst into tears. It had taken her one hundred and fifty-two years of Halo Awareness Classes to get even a faint glimmer started, and now that had gone. And all because Gaby had made her come to earth!

'Sshh . . .' Gaby lifted the hem of her nightie and offered it to Angie to wipe her eyes. 'The girls are looking at us.'

That was a bit of an understatement. Every member of Form 1C had turned and was staring at the two angels with a jaw-dropped, can't-believe-what-I'm-seeing face.

'Pull yourself together,' Gaby said briskly. 'They're coming over. Try and act normally.'

'B-but what *is* normally?' asked poor Angie.

'Just try to be like them,' replied Gaby, not thinking how difficult that was when everyone else had ordinary haircuts and was wearing a yellow and purple uniform, and you'd got long ringlets like sausages and were wearing a white nightie. Most of all, it was difficult to look like a schoolgirl if you'd got two small, feathery wings sticking out of your back.

Luckily, the two angels had appeared on the far side of the playground, so Form 1C took a moment or two to get over to them. There was enough time for Gaby to quickly tuck her own wings, then Angie's, into the neat openings at the back of their nighties.

Form 1C surrounded them, wide-eyed and wondering.

'Who are you?'

'What are you doing here?'

'Why are you dressed like that?'

'When did you arrive?'

'You look like *dolls*!'

Angie and Gaby didn't speak. Angie because she was too scared, Gaby because she hadn't quite made up her mind how to explain their sudden appearance.

'Hang on, hang on!' a small girl with dark hair broke through the crowd. 'They can't answer ten questions at once. Give them a bit of space.'

She moved everyone back a little. 'Now,' she said, 'I'm Julia. What are your names?'

'I'm Gaby and this is Angie,' said Gaby, hoping that no bits of wing were showing.

'Term started on Monday,' Julia said. 'We thought all the new girls had arrived. Where on earth have you come from?'

'Oh, from nowhere on *earth*,' Angie said, suddenly finding her voice. 'We're from –'

Gaby poked Angie. 'We're from a remote place you've probably never heard of,' she interrupted. 'It's very warm there – that's why we're dressed like this.'

'Is that your national costume, then?' asked a slim girl with gingery hair.

Gaby nodded. She'd read a few books in heaven, and picked up other bits of information from the glimpse of earth she'd had through the viewing mirror, but she wasn't quite sure what national costume was. 'We came straight from there this morning and haven't had time to change our clothes,' she added.

'Did you fly?' asked the gingery girl, whose name was Marcy.

'Oh yes,' said Angie immediately, glad to be truthful.

'British Airways, I expect,' said another girl.

'No, we used our wings,' said Angie, and was immediately poked in the ribs again by Gaby.

'Angie likes a joke!' Gaby said quickly.

Marcy pointed at their feet. 'You haven't even got shoes!'

'You don't need shoes when you fly,' Angie said.

The girls frowned, then Julia's face cleared. 'I expect she means because of those little fold-up slippers they give you on the plane.'

'Yes, that's right,' Gaby said, while Angie just looked confused.

'Where's your luggage, then?' asked Nicola, a plumpish girl with glasses.

'Luggage?' Gaby said, stumped for a moment.

'All your bags, bits and pieces . . .'

'They didn't get lost, did they?' Julia asked.

'We didn't have —' began Angie.

'That's right!' Gaby agreed with Julia quickly.

'All lost. Every bit.'

'How awful!' said Nicola.

Marcy frowned. 'This is all very strange,' she said. 'You look so *weird* – and I never heard of any place on earth where people wear nighties for national dress.'

'Well, wherever they come from they won't be able to stay in those nighties,' Nicola said. 'Someone had better take them to Matron to get kitted out.'

'I'll do that!' Julia said quickly. 'And we'd better go now – before next class. Tell Miss Bunce I'll be a bit late, will you?'

She took an angel in each hand and led them across the playground towards the main school building. 'I'm glad you've come,' she said as they went inside. 'You seem sort of different from every-one else.'

'We're different because we're from –' Angie began.

'Nevaeh!' Gaby put in quickly.

Angie looked shocked. 'Why did you say that?'

18

she angel-whispered to Gaby.  'Why do you keep telling lies?'

'That wasn't a real lie – Nevaeh is just heaven spelt backwards,' Gaby whispered back.

'Well, *I'm* not telling any lies,' Angie said. 'If I do, I'll lose my halo for ever.'

Julia led them up two sets of stairs and along a corridor to Matron's room. She knocked on the door and they went in.

Matron, plump as a winter duvet, was sitting with her feet up on a settee. She had a large box of chocolates in one hand and a book in the other. She stared at the angels

❋   Angels are able to whisper very, very quietly indeed, so that no human can hear.

19

and the angels stared at her.

'Is this a matron?' Angie asked. 'Why is she so *big?*'

Gaby coughed to try and hide what Angie was saying, but luckily Matron was munching too loudly to hear her.

'Good gracious!' she said, stopping in the act of popping a cherry twirl into her mouth. 'Twins in long white frocks!'

'Oh, I never thought. *Are* you twins?' Julia asked.

Gaby shook her head. 'Just . . . er . . . sisters,' she said.

Angie nodded approvingly. *'We are all sisters under the skin,'* she said, and angel-whispered, 'I learnt that at Halo Awareness Classes eighty-six years ago.'

Matron looked from the chocolates to the angels and back, then popped in a walnut whirl. 'Where are your trunks and cases? Where are your proper clothes?'

'That's just it,' Julia said. 'Everything they had is

lost – all their clothes. They came straight from the airport in just what they're wearing.'

'Dear, oh dear – those airlines!' Matron said vaguely. She waved a hand towards a vast cupboard. 'Borrow what you like in the way of clothes, dearies.' She paused, torn between a toffee and a mint cream, then said to Julia, 'Is there room in your dormie for them?'

Julia turned from the cupboard to nod, and Matron said, 'You can have them in with you, then.' She picked up both chocolates at the same time and put them in her mouth. 'Take what you want – shoes as well,' she mumbled, 'and then off you go.'

Six arms reached towards the big cupboard and a few moments later Angie, Gaby and Julia, their arms full of clothes, were making their way towards one of the First Year dorms.

'I *hoped* she'd say you could sleep in my dorm!' Julia said. 'I'll show you around – we'll have a laugh!'

'Um . . . um . . .' Gaby said, chewing.

'Gaby!' said Angie. 'You're not eating one of those round brown things!'

Gaby licked her lips. 'Yes, I am,' she said, 'and it was . . .' she winked at Angie, '*heavenly*.'

3

Gaby Goes for a
Quick Flit

Julia led them up a winding stone staircase. 'Our
dorm's right at the top of this tower,' she said. 'It's
really nice, and we're well away from anyone else
here. Miss Bunce has got her own study room on
the floor below.'

'Who's Miss Bunce?' Gaby asked.

'Don't you even know the name of our teacher?!'
Julia said. She grinned. 'Well, she's *supposed* to be
our teacher, but half the time she doesn't seem to
know which way up she is.'

'Oh,' Angie said, very surprised. 'Does she fly,

then? It *is* difficult to work out what way up you are when you start, isn't it? I mean, when you've got clouds above you and clouds below you it's hard to tell.'

Julia stared at her. 'What do you mean?'

'You big girl's nightie!' Gaby angel-whispered to Angie. 'Of course Miss Bunce doesn't fly! Only *we* can do that.' She said to Julia, 'Angie's so *funny*, isn't she?'

Julia, feeling a bit confused, laughed. She pushed open the door of a big, round room with ten beds in it. 'The two beds by the window are free,' she said. 'And you can have the cupboards next to them for all your bits and pieces.' She pulled a sympathetic face. 'When they eventually get here, that is.'

Gaby bounced down on one of the beds, her arms still full of clothes. 'This one will do me,' she said.

Angie tried the mattress of the other bed. 'It's a bit hard,' she said, then muttered to herself, 'but I suppose it would be, after clouds . . .'

Julia, luckily, didn't hear her. She jumped on to

her own bed. 'We might as well skip class and just doss about for the rest of the day,' she said. 'Why don't you start lessons properly tomorrow?'

'Sounds all right to me,' Gaby said.

'Don't you want to change out of those things and put on your uniform?' Julia asked. 'Not being funny, but they do make you look odd. You look like those china dolls you see in antique shops.'

She started sorting through the pile of clothes. 'I don't suppose you'll want all this stuff,' she said, dishing out jumpers, blouses and skirts to the angels. 'We seem to have got about twelve of everything here.' She shook out a vest and held it up. 'I'm sure you won't want *these*. I hate wearing vests underneath everything, don't you?'

Gaby looked at it and her face brightened.

'Oh no, we *love* wearing vests,' she said.

'Do we?' Angie asked in surprise.

'Of course,' Gaby said. 'We wear them all the time. We never take them off!' In an angel-whisper she added, 'They'll hide our wings!'

Julia raised her eyebrows. 'Oh, I suppose it's the custom where you come from.'

Gaby nodded and just then, the door was pushed open slightly and the school cat walked in.

Gaby and Angie gave a shriek.

'What's that?!' Gaby said.

'Is it a devil?' asked Angie, jumping on to her bed.

Julia looked at them both in amazement, and then her face cleared. 'Oh, I see. It's another of your jokes.'

'No! It . . . it's because we don't have those things where we come from,' said Gaby.

'You don't have *animals*?' asked Julia incredulously.

Gaby thought for a moment. She'd heard that there were two unicorns in heaven, but she'd never seen them. 'Not those sort,' she said.

'You don't have cats? I thought cats were everywhere in the world.'

🌟 In heaven Level Six, where Gaby and Angie come from, there are no animals.

'Everywhere except Nevaeh,' Gaby said.

'Cats are lovely,' Julia said. 'Tiblet!' she called, and the large tabby cat came to her and was lifted on to the bed. 'There are three cats in the school – and they're all quite harmless!' she added, seeing that Angie was still looking scared. 'They're kept to catch the mice.'

'Ah,' said Gaby, and angel-whispered to Angie, 'and don't you dare ask what *mice* are.'

The cat jumped, purring, from bed to bed.

'He's not really supposed to be in here,' Julia said. 'But I don't see why he can't break the rules – everyone else does.'

'What do you mean?' Gaby asked.

'Well, it's a dippy sort of school. Our Maths teacher is really strict, but the others are a pushover. Either they're dead on their feet –'

'Dead on their feet?!' Angie and Gaby squealed together.

'Really old, I mean,' said Julia, looking at them oddly, 'or they're so scatty they're completely out of it. No one seems to care whether we learn anything or not.'

Gaby began wandering around the dorm, touching things, looking at photographs and posters, sniffing a drum of talcum powder here, shaking a bottle of lemonade there. There were so many interesting things, she thought. So many different shapes and sizes and feels, so many colours. Angie, meanwhile, was trying to get her legs into the arms of a purple school jumper.

'Not like that!' Gaby angel-whispered, luckily turning to see her before Julia did.

'You put it over your head!'

Angie giggled and pulled it off quickly while Julia was still playing with the cat.

Gaby went over to the window and looked out. She managed to open the catch, and leant over the low window sill.

'We're not really supposed to do that,' Julia said. 'I think they're frightened we'll fall out. We're quite high up here, you see.'

Gaby hung right out of the window. 'We're not that high!' she said, looking down four floors to the grass below. 'What's at the bottom?'

'The library's on the ground floor,' Julia began, and then she hesitated and looked anxious. 'You'd better not lean out any further, it might be dangerous.'

'I think I can see some of the other girls,' Gaby said, standing on tiptoe. 'Hang on. If I just stretch . . . *oops*!' And she stretched just that bit too far and tumbled over the edge of the window sill!

Julia gave a scream, standing horror-struck in the middle of the room. 'Your sister – she's fallen out of the window!' she shouted to Angie. 'Oh, what shall we do?!' Too frightened to look out in case she saw something gruesome, she ran to the door and flung it open.

'Oh, help, someone!' she screamed, stumbling down the stairs. 'Call a doctor! Ambulance! The new girl's fallen out of the window!'

Are Beefburgers Better than Angel Cake?

Julia ran down the staircase as fast as she could, frantic and almost sobbing with panic. The new girl had fallen out of the window – and it was all her fault! She should have looked after her better!

Behind her came Angie, walking quite slowly and thinking how like Gaby to do something silly. She was always getting up to tricks like that in heaven – leaping from cloud to cloud or free-falling from one level to another.

Julia crashed through the door at the bottom of the tower and raced towards what, she was certain, was the lifeless body of Gaby.

'I'm frightened to look!' she called to Angie in a trembly voice. 'I just know she's going to be horribly, horribly hurt. Perhaps she'll even be de—'

Rounding the corner, she stopped so suddenly that Angie cannoned into her. She stopped because standing on the grass, perfectly well and whole, was Gaby, who'd just finished folding back her wings into her nightie.

'Beat you down!' Gaby said.

Julia, white-faced and panting, stared at her. 'I . . . I don't understand. How d-did you get down without hurting yourself?'

Gaby didn't reply. She stood on tiptoe to look through the downstairs window. 'So this is your library, is it?'

'B-but what did you –'

Angie joined Gaby at the window. 'Ooh! Hundreds of books!'

'Thousands of books!' Gaby said.

Julia shook her head in bewilderment.

'You couldn't possibly have fallen all that way

without breaking something!' she burst out. 'You haven't got a scratch! There's not a mark or bruise on you!' She began to back off in fright. 'There's something funny going on. You've played a trick on me. I don't understand . . .'

Gaby sighed. She hadn't *meant* to fall out of the window. In fact she hadn't meant to use her wings at all while she was on earth. Wings, she felt, would be a bit of a give-away.

'Look, don't go off,' she said to Julia. She shot a look at Angie. 'I think we'll have to tell her the truth, you know.'

Angie smiled happily. *'Tell the truth, seek the light, It makes your halo nice and bright!'* she said. 'We learnt that at Halo Aware—'

'Yes, yes, not now,' said Gaby impatiently.

'But how did you do it?' asked Julia, more bewildered than ever. 'How did you fall out of that window and not get hurt?'

'Well,' Gaby said. 'If you really want to know – I flew.'

'Flew! What do you mean?!'

Gaby and Angie looked at each other.

'The thing is . . .' Angie began.

'Not to beat about the bush . . .' put in Gaby.

'We're not actually girls as *such*.'

'We're actually . . .'

'Angels!' they said together.

There was a stunned silence from Julia.

'See!' Gaby said, dropping her nightie over her shoulder and showing a few downy feathers. 'Wings and everything!'

Julia still didn't speak.

'And I used to have a halo,' Angie said, looking at Gaby rather indignantly.

Julia sat down on the grass. 'How *can* you be angels?' she asked faintly. 'Are you both dead, then?'

'Of course not!' Angie said.

'We were dead once,' Gaby said carelessly, 'but not now. Now we're angels.'

'So that's why you . . . you look like that – with the ringlets and nighties and everything?'

Gaby and Angie nodded. 'This is how angels look,' Gaby said.

'But –' Just as Julia was going to start asking questions, a loud bell sounded and both angels put their hands to their ears.

'Awful noise!' Gaby said.

'Bells in heaven don't clang like that!' said Angie.

'It's the school bell,' said Julia, still staring wonderingly from one angel to the other. 'It means lessons are over for the day.'

Girls started streaming out into the grounds.

Gaby said, 'Look, you won't say anything to the

others about us, will you?'

Julia shook her head slowly. 'Of course not. They'd never believe me! Besides, if people find out about you it'll be crazy. You'll be taken away and investigated – put in a cage or something.'

'Hear that, Angie?' Gaby asked sternly.

'Look,' went on Julia rather anxiously. 'Let's go back upstairs now, before all the others come in, so you can get into school uniform and look more normal by the time we go to tea.'

Angie and Gaby nodded. 'I'll fly back up, shall I?' Gaby asked, grinning wickedly.

'Don't you dare!' said Julia.

Julia surveyed Gaby and Angie, pleased with herself. None of the other First Years had come up to the dorm, so she'd had a good half-hour to work on the angels.

'You look all right,' she said, pulling down Gaby's jumper a little and adjusting Angie's tie. 'You look almost human!'

'Just remember to keep your vest on all the

time,' Gaby said to Angie.

'You can say you catch cold easily or you've got weak chests or something,' suggested Julia. She looked at her watch. 'Shall we go down to eat? I'm starving!'

Gaby and Angie followed Julia down the staircase. When they reached the bottom and the main block of the school, a crowd of other girls began to stream along with them, all talking and chattering and laughing.

Angie pulled her ringlets round her ears in an effort to drown out the noise. 'So *loud*,' she complained. 'What a row!'

'We're not used to it,' Gaby said to Julia. 'The only time we ever hear a mass of people together is at heavenly choir practice – and they certainly don't sound like *that*.'

The three of them entered the dining hall, where the noise was even greater.

Rows and rows of tables and benches criss-crossed the room and at the top was a long serving counter.

'What do we do here?' Gaby asked, staring about her.

'Eat, of course!' Julia said. 'Breakfast, lunch and tea. Three times a day we're in here; the staff have their own –'

'Three times a day!' both angels interrupted.

Julia looked at them. 'How often do you eat in hea . . . in Nevaeh, then?'

'Once a day,' Angie said, greedily eyeing the

39

plates of food going by. 'We have a small bowl of milk and honey at dawn.'

'Is that all?'

'And a slice of angel cake on Sundays,' Gaby said.

'But you should eat more than that!' Julia said. 'Food gives you energy.'

'You don't need energy to sit on a cloud all day,' Gaby said.

'But you need to eat to live!' Julia protested and then she thought about what she was saying and giggled. 'Oh, I see!'

She showed the angels where to get a tray, and picked out a beefburger and salad for each of them. 'First Years all sit together,' she said. 'Our table is at the bottom of the hall.'

Angie had bitten into her beefburger before

40

they'd even sat down. 'It's *lovely*!' she said. 'How many can we have?'

'Mmm. Gorgeous. So tasty!' Gaby said, trying hers and licking her lips. 'What's it called?'

'It's a beefburger,' Julia whispered, hoping none of the other girls would hear.

'What's a beefburger?' asked Gaby.

Julia shrugged. 'Sort of minced beef and stuff.'

'What's a beef?' Angie put in.

'Beef comes from an animal that's –'

Gaby and Angie both suddenly spat out their beefburgers.

'An *animal*?!' Gaby said.

'We're eating a *cat*?!' Angie cried.

'No, no!' Julia said hastily. 'It's a different sort of animal. A very big one specially grown for eating.'

But Gaby and Angie had pushed

their beefburgers to one side and were now eating salad.

Julia looked round the table. Marcy, Nicola and the others were staring, open-mouthed, at the angels.

'They're . . . er . . . vegetarians,' Julia explained. 'They took beefburgers by mistake. They'd never seen one before.'

'Never seen a beefburger before?' Marcy asked incredulously.

Angie had stopped eating again, a small tomato halfway to her mouth. 'Excuse me,' she said to Julia, 'but is this round red thing also an animal?'

There was a stunned silence from the rest of the First Year girls, then Marcy said, 'What the hell does she mean?'

'Bless you!' both angels said together.✻

'Why did you say that?' Julia asked. 'No one sneezed.'

'No,' Marcy said, 'I was just saying what the hell –'

✻ Whenever anyone says the word 'hell', angels are programmed to say 'Bless you'.

42

'Bless you!' cried the angels.

Marcy made a twirly movement round her head to indicate that she thought they must be dippy.

Gaby moved closer to Julia. 'We can't help it,' she whispered. 'We have to say *bless you* if anyone mentions that word.'

'D'you mean *hell*?'

'Bless you!' both chorused again.

Julia looked round at the table of astonished girls, wondering how she was going to cover this up. 'Atishoo! Atishoo!' she suddenly exploded. She gave a false laugh. 'Fancy,' she said, 'Gaby and Angie knew I was going to sneeze before *I* did!'

No one spoke, and then Marcy shook her head. 'Mark my words,' she said darkly, 'there is something *very* strange about those two new girls . . .'

After supper, some of the First Years went to their common room, but Gaby and Angie were so exhausted (it was the first time they'd actually *done* anything in over two hundred years) they crept into their beds and slept soundly all night.

5

Miss Bunce Takes a Nap

'Look, leave all the talking to me,' Gaby said to Angie on the way into Miss Bunce's class the following morning.

'But what if she asks me anything?' Angie said.

'You can reply but don't say anything *silly*.'

'Well, I'm certainly not telling any lies,' said Angie.

Julia beckoned to them from the other side of the classroom. 'Over here,' she said. 'Come and sit at the back. Miss Bunce is so daffy she might not even notice you.'

Gaby and Angie sat at a double desk and Julia sat on the other side of the gangway.

After a moment Angie got up and started carefully folding the pleats in her skirt before sitting on them again. Even though she was on earth, she didn't intend to let her standards slip.

'You mustn't say anything silly,' Gaby continued, 'because we don't want Miss Bunce to start wondering about us and investigating us.' She looked at Angie sternly. 'You don't want to be investigated – you wouldn't like it. And you want to stay on earth, don't you?'

Angie wrinkled her nose. 'Stay here for ever, you mean?'

'Maybe,' Gaby said.

'And never get my halo back?'

'What good's a *halo* to anyone?' Gaby said. 'Look, would you rather be down here doing things and having fun, or sitting on a cloud for years on end, waiting for something to happen?'

Angie thought deeply. 'I think . . . down here having fun,' she said after a long moment.

'I should jolly well think so,' said Gaby, rather relieved.

'But he'll be very cross, won't he?' Angie said.

'Who?'

'The Archangel. He'll try to get us back.'

'Oh, he might not bother,' said Gaby. 'He's very busy, is old Holy Joe.'

'Who's Holy Joe?' Marcy asked curiously, turning to face the angels from the seat in front.

'Er . . . our uncle. Our uncle Joe,' Gaby said. She ignored Angie's reproachful look. 'Uncle Joe didn't really want us to come here,' she said by way of explanation.

'Is Uncle Joe your guardian, then?' Marcy asked.

'Oh no!' Angie said, jumping in before Gaby could stop her. 'He's not a *guardian* angel!'

Marcy frowned. 'I don't understand what you're talking about half the time,' she said, and added spitefully, 'There's something about you two which isn't quite right. I'm going to keep my eye on you and –'

Luckily, just at that moment, Miss Bunce came in. Unluckily, she was feeling quite *un*daffy that morning, so spotted the two angels straightaway.

Miss Bunce had been at the convent for so long, the authorities had forgotten she was still there. She frequently forgot she was there herself. Wearing an ancient green dress topped with an assortment of scarves and fringed shawls, she peered at the angels through round wire glasses.

'I don't recognise you!' she said. 'I think you must be in the wrong class.'

Gaby, prompted by a prod from Julia, stood up. 'Please – we are First Years, but we arrived late.'

Miss Bunce blinked at her vaguely. 'But I wasn't informed of this. I wasn't told I was going to have two extra girls.'

Gaby gave Miss Bunce a full, radiant smile. 'We're so sorry to be late arriving,' she said softly.

'We do hope it hasn't inconvenienced you at all,'

Angie cooed, looking at her from under long golden lashes. 'Are you feeling daffy this morning?'

The class started giggling but Miss Bunce, who was slightly deaf and who'd thought Angie had asked whether or not she was *happy*, was completely won over.

'Dear girls. Delightful manners,' the class heard her murmur. 'That's perfectly all right,' she said to the angels. 'Don't give it another thought.' She began to distribute books around the class. 'Quiet reading today, I think.'

'What, *again?*' a voice in the class was heard to say.

'Please turn to chapter two of *Spookspotting*,' said Miss Bunce.

'We read that on Friday,' the same voice complained.

'And Thursday,' added someone else.

'How well you will know it, then!' Miss Bunce cried. 'Now read twelve pages quietly to yourselves while I get on with some important work of my own.' And she got out her beaded lace milk-jug

covers, which were always a hit at the St Winifred's
Christmas Fayres.

'Is this *lessons*?' Angie whispered to Gaby, as
around them girls either yawned and dozed off, or
got out comic books to read.

'Not sure,' answered Gaby, looking around. She
turned to Julia and held up the book she'd been
given. 'What's this *Spookspotting* about?'

'Oh, it's about a girl who goes to stay in an old
house and hunts for ghosts.'

'What's ghosts?' Angie asked.

'The Archangel mentioned them,' Gaby added.

'Well, I've never seen one,' Julia said, 'but
apparently they're people who once lived on earth,
who haunt places. You can see through them and
they can walk through walls and float in the air
and . . .'

'Poof!' Gaby said. 'We can do that.'

'We can't walk through walls!' Angie said.

'We can float in the air!' Gaby boasted. 'We can
float *brilliantly*. You watch!'

And before they could stop her she'd slipped past

Miss Bunce (who was doing a tricky bit of beading and didn't notice) and gone out of the classroom into the corridor.

There was a small glass window in the door and she waved to Angie and Julia through it. After a second or two they saw her yellow shirt go by, then her purple skirt, and then a pair of feet encased in sturdy brown school shoes, doing little kick-steps in the air through the small window.

When Gaby came back in she was smiling hugely. 'We can do anything ghosts can do!' she said.

Julia looked around the classroom; she didn't

50

think anyone else had seen. 'I believe you,' she said, 'but I wish you wouldn't do things like that!'

For the next forty minutes Miss Bunce worked tirelessly, beading and threading, while the class did their own thing. Angie and Gaby got down to some work with Julia, who was bringing them

up to date on pop music.🌠

'I do hope you've enjoyed your first class,' Miss Bunce said to the angels when the end-of-lesson bell went.

'Oh, we have!' said Gaby.

Angie added, 'Thank you so much, Miss Bunce. It's been most interesting learning about the top ten.'

'Charmed, I'm sure . . .' Miss Bunce murmured vaguely.

Angie was last to leave the classroom. Just as she was passing Miss Bunce's chair, a gentle hand was placed on her shoulder. 'Just a minute, my dear. I must take you both to the secretary so that your details can be entered on the school register.'

Julia looked round quickly. 'I'll take them if you like, Miss Bunce!'

'No, that's quite all right,' Miss Bunce said. 'I'll just gather up my things and we'll go now.'

🌠 In heaven the only music is from heavenly choirs and harps.

Julia looked at Gaby in a panic. 'Do something!'

'Don't worry,' Gaby said, and she whispered to Angie, '*Angel dust!*' ✻

Both angels reached into their skirt pockets, blew on their palms and puffed something into Miss Bunce's face. She'd been about to get up, but she immediately slumped forward on to the desk, a gentle smile crossing her features. She began to snore quietly.

Julia stared at her. 'What have you done?!'

'Oh, just sent her off for a while,' Gaby said.

'It's angel dust,' Angie explained. 'Angels always have some on them.'

'But where does it come from?' Julia asked.

'I don't really know,' Angie said with a shrug. 'It's just always in our pockets.'

'Like you have fluff,' explained Gaby. She took the register from the limp hand of Miss Bunce. 'We'd better fill this in,' she said. 'When she wakes

✻ Angels always have angel dust in their pockets, in case they have to get crying cherubs off to sleep.

up she'll think she took us to the secretary. What do we have to put in?'

'Just your full name and address, I think,' Julia said, and together they wrote:

Gabrielle and Angela Paradise
Level 6, Sky Heights
Cloud Crescent
Fluffytown
Nevaeh

Which more or less satisfied Angie, being more or less the truth.

6

A Lesson with a Nothing

That afternoon, the angels were both in front of the bathroom mirror. Gaby was struggling to get her hair *out* of ringlets, while Angie was struggling to keep hers *in*.

'What are you doing?' Angie asked, twirling a final perfect ringlet round her finger. 'What's that yukky stuff?'

'Hair gel,' Gaby replied. 'Julia gave it to me.' She squeezed the tube and slicked a long column of it on to her hair, then dragged her hair flat to her head. It immediately sprang out again.

'No matter what I do,' Gaby said despairingly, 'it *will* keep jumping back into ringlets.'

'That's because we're angels,' Angie said, pinching her cheeks to make them glow. She fastened a pink ribbon bow on the side of her head. 'We can't help looking pretty. That's how we're supposed to look. *Hair curled, eyes bright — Angels always look just right*!' she quoted.

'I don't want to look pretty!' said Gaby crossly, clamping a row of clips round her head.

'Ooh, such a naughty cross face!' said Angie. 'If the Archangel could see you now . . .'

'I dreamt of Holy Joe last night,' Gaby said.

'I wish you wouldn't call him that!' Angie said fearfully. 'I'm sure it's against the rules.'

'I dreamt I sat up and saw him in the wardrobe mirror,' Gaby went on. 'He was just standing there saying, "*You cannot stay . . . you must return*."'

Angie shivered. 'Perhaps it wasn't a dream!'

'Of course it was!' said Gaby, although actually she wasn't quite sure whether she'd dreamt it, or if it had been real.

She looked in the bathroom mirror, groaned, and removed the clips. Ringlets, stiff with gel, sprang out from each side of her head. She turned away in disgust. Even in school uniform, she couldn't help looking like an angel.

Angie inspected her nails and blew a speck of dust from her shoulder. 'Our lesson this afternoon is with a nothing,' she said.

Gaby snorted. 'How can you have a lesson with a *nothing*?'

'That's what Julia told me!' Angie said indignantly. 'That's exactly what she said.'

'This class is a doddle,' Julia said as they sat waiting for the teacher to arrive. 'Sister Bertha is even more out of it than Miss Bunce is.'

'Will it be more quiet reading?' Angie asked.

Julia shook her head. 'Sister Bertha does religious knowledge,' she said. 'At least, she's supposed to. She's so doddery, though, she usually falls asleep ten minutes after she's done the register.'

Gaby gave a squeal as the door opened and a

small figure dressed from head to toe in black entered the room. 'Oh, wow!' she said. 'What's that?'

'Is this the nothing?' asked Angie excitedly.

'Ssh! She'll hear you,' Julia giggled. 'She's a *nun*. Spelt NUN.'

'Well, that's nearly what I said,' Angie said. 'But why have we got a person like her?'

'Because this is a convent school – lots of the teachers are nuns,' Julia explained. 'They're all called Sister Something-or-other.'

'All called Sister Something-or-other?' Angie asked. 'How strange. How do you know which one you're talking about then?'

Julia sighed. 'I don't mean they're actually called *something-or-other*,' she said, 'I mean –'

'It's OK,' Gaby interrupted. 'I'll explain it to her later.'

Sister Bertha called the register, then yawned deeply and slowly. 'This afternoon, dear girls, I'm going to talk to you about heaven,' she said.

There were a few answering yawns from around the class, but Julia kicked the angels' desk and the three of them sat up straight and looked at each other.

'Now, girls,' Sister Bertha said gently, 'we don't know much about heaven, but we *do* know that it's like a beautiful garden.'

'Excuse *me*!' said Angie indignantly, and was nudged to be quiet by Gaby.

'All manner of wonderful flowers grow there,' Sister Bertha went on, her voice growing warm

and gushy.
'Little birds fly in the trees . . . wild animals walk unharmed among the flowers.'

Angie's ringlets bounced. 'There aren't any wild animals!' she announced.

'You mustn't interrupt, little one,' Sister Bertha said gently. 'Now, all the birds and the beasts in heaven live happily together, the lions walk with the lambs and –'

'There aren't any animals at all!' Angie protested. 'Or trees or flowers or birds! There's nothing except clouds.'

'Sssh . . .' said Gaby, as everyone in the class turned round to look at Angie.

'I'm afraid you are sadly misguided, my child,' Sister Bertha said softly, 'and you really mustn't interrupt when I'm speaking.'

'But what you're saying is all wrong!' Angie said.

Gaby groaned inwardly. She knew she could blow angel dust in Angie's eyes to shut her up, but wouldn't the class think it odd if Angie suddenly slumped on to her desk and started snoring?

'Do be quiet!' she angel-whispered. 'If you go on like this they'll find out about us and then we'll be taken away and investigated.'

'But they ought to know the truth about heaven!' Angie protested, getting to her feet. 'You see,' she went on earnestly to Sister Bertha, 'it's not like that at all — not lions and lambs walking together.'

'My child,' Sister Bertha intoned, 'I'm afraid you are wrong. Haven't you seen the wonderful paintings of heaven by the Old Masters?'

'No, I haven't,' Angie said. 'But anyway, how would the Old Masters know? They haven't been there, have they? They weren't dead when they painted them.'

'No, but . . .' Sister Bertha wagged a finger at Angie. 'You mustn't contradict me like this. If you're naughty and disobedient, you won't go to heaven!'

'As a matter of fact . . .' Angie began hotly, but Gaby gave her skirt a sharp tug.

Sister Bertha looked round the class. 'Well, what do you other dear girls think? Has anyone a different idea about heaven? I think we could have a very interesting discussion.'

Marcy stood up. 'I think it will be like a great big health club,' she said. 'It'll have a huge heated swimming pool with palm trees and vines hanging over it, and you'd be able to go swimming about, eating grapes at the same time.'

'I don't think it'll be like that!' Nicola said. 'I think it'll be a place where everything's made of chocolate and you can just eat and eat as much as you like all day without feeling sick.'

'No, it won't,' Sarah said. 'It's just lots of people being nice to each other. It's the sort of place where you could be passing through a door at the same time as someone else, and you could stand there for *years* going, "After you," and the other person saying, "No, after you," and then you going, "No, I insist," and the other person saying, "No really – after you," until you're blue in the face.'

Everyone laughed.

'I think,' Susie said, 'that it's all glittering with gold and jewels and you'd have amazing bedrooms with everything you wanted in them and you'd just have to wish to get every present you ever wanted. It would be like having a birthday every day.'

Gaby had her hand firmly across Angie's mouth all this time, but she'd been wriggling and struggling to make herself heard.

'It's nothing like that!' she burst out. 'It's just clouds. Clouds, clouds and more clouds. Squillions of clouds going on for ever!'

The girls turned to look at her scornfully.

'It couldn't be like *that*,' Nicola said. 'That

would be so boring! Don't you think so, Sister Bertha?'

'I think,' Sister Bertha began in a muzzy voice, 'that we . . . we . . . zzzzzz.' And she was asleep, her head drooping on to the starched white of her front.

'Look at that!' Gaby whispered, 'and all without angel dust.'

'She's off!' Julia said. 'Let's go into the common room and play some music.'

Everyone was back in class by the time the bell for end of lessons went.

Sister Bertha, refreshed by her nap, sat up and looked around her brightly. 'Well, we've had a lovely talk about heaven, girls. I think you all enjoyed it, didn't you?'

The class gave an enthusiastic murmur.

'You all look most revitalised – and that's what I often find: talk of heaven does revive one, while thoughts of hell –'

'Bless you!' both angels chorused.

'But I didn't –'

'Atishoo!' Julia shouted desperately. 'Come on, everyone, time for tea!'

7

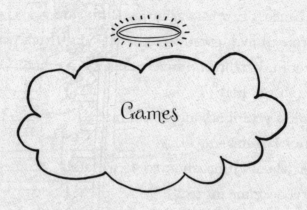

Games

'You mean we've got to put
these on?' Gaby asked.
'These tiny little knicker
things?'

'They're shorts,' Julia
said.

'They certainly are!'
Angie said, and
added in a shocked
voice, 'We're going
to show all our legs.'

'You wear them so you can run better,' Julia explained. 'If you wear shorts you've got more freedom to run and jump and play games and everything. And we wear T-shirt tops and light shoes with them.'

'I'll be glad to get out of this jumper!' said Gaby with relief, scratching her arms. 'It itches like mad.'

'So does this skirt!' Angie said. 'I feel as if I'm wearing an animal!'

The three of them got changed and went into the gym before the rest of the class arrived. Julia showed them all the equipment and explained what they'd have to do on it.

'We have to climb to the top of those ropes, one

hand over the other – it's really difficult,' she said.

'Pshaw!' said Gaby scornfully. 'That's easy!' And she wriggled her shoulders so that her wings slithered themselves out from beneath her vest and T-shirt. She flapped them once . . . twice and reached the top of the ropes, then glided across the wall bars and hung off the top rung, grinning at the other two.

Angie frowned. 'I wish you wouldn't keep showing off,' she said. 'It's strictly against the rules. Angels never –'

'We're not angels at the moment,' Gaby said, 'we're girls. Anyway, there's no one around.'

'There will be soon,' Julia said, 'and Marcy's already very suspicious of you.'

'I'm suspicious of *her*,' Gaby said. 'I don't like her.'

'No, she's not very nice, is she?' Julia said. 'She's a bit of a cat.'

A little while later (after Gaby had tucked in her wings), the rest of the class came in, followed by Sister Teresa, the teacher who was taking them for Games. She was one of the youngest of the nuns and was very bouncy and jolly. She didn't get changed out of her habit for gym, but rushed about with it tossed over her arm, directing the girls around the equipment and urging them on.

After half-an-hour's warming up (Sister Teresa was pleased with the way the angels leapt over the box – she said they practically flew over it) the girls were told to get their hockey sticks and boots and go outside.

'Hockey's a game,' Julia whispered as everyone got into their heavy boots. 'There are two teams, and the object is to knock a ball into the other team's goal.'

'Why?' Gaby asked.

Julia shrugged. 'Don't ask me.'

'But why should anyone bother if a ball gets knocked into their goal?'

'I don't know,' Julia said. 'That's just the game.'

Gaby shook her head wonderingly. 'How funny!'

Julia noticed that Angie was standing in front of Marcy, staring at her. 'Come over here, Angie!' she called. 'You haven't got your boots on yet.'

She came. Angie usually did as she was told. 'Why were you staring at Marcy?' Gaby asked curiously.

'I was looking for whiskers,' Angie said.

'What?'

'Whiskers or fur or a tail,' Angie said. 'Julia said she was a bit of a cat – I wanted to see which bit.'

'It doesn't mean *that*!' Julia said.

Sister Teresa ran past them in trainers, her black-and-white headdress at an odd angle. 'Get cracking, you girls!' she called. 'On with the boots and out on the field!'

Once everyone was out, Sister Teresa picked the teams.

'Nicola can be centre back,' she said, 'and you, Julia, will be goalie, as usual. You two new girls – now, where shall we put you? You look quite light on your feet.'

'We are!' Angie said, 'because we're –'

'Could they play as wings?' interrupted Julia, with a wink at the two angels.

'Ooh, yes, we'd like to be *wings*!' Gaby said.

'We'd be very good as *wings*,' Angie put in with a giggle, so Sister Teresa agreed that they could play in that position.

They started off well enough, but after ten minutes of racing about after the ball, both angels were fed up. They were fast enough on their feet, but they couldn't see the point of the game; they really couldn't care whether their team won or not.

'I hate these heavy boots!' Angie complained. 'I think it's miserable how everyone has to wear shoes down here!'

'I hate these shorts, my legs are freezing,' grumbled Gaby. 'And I can't stand all this running about! I'm not used to it – it's such a waste of time when you can fly.'

Angie suddenly squealed excitedly and pointed. 'Look!' she called to Gaby. 'Teeny weeny angels. Two of them on that flower!'

Gaby looked. 'I don't think they can be angels,' she said. 'Even the seraphim don't have coloured wings like that – and they're *never* that small.'

Sarah ran by, waving her hockey stick. 'Oh, look at those two butterflies!' she said. 'Red Admirals by the look of them – they're late!'

Gaby and Angie looked at each other. 'Butterflies,' Gaby said. 'They must be a bit like animals, then. But different.'

'Smaller and not furry,' added Angie.

'Girls! You two playing in the wing position!' Sister Teresa called down the field. 'Are you part of this game or are you just chatting?'

'Just chatting,' Angie said.

'I hate running about with these sticks and

balls!' Gaby sighed.

'I can't see the point of *games*,' Angie said with a sigh of her own and then, remembering, said, 'Oops, shouldn't have done that!'✻

'We'd better be careful,' Gaby said.

'Unless . . .' Angie said daringly, 'We could . . . you know . . .'

'Of course!' Gaby said, and she heaved the most forlorn sigh.

'Aahhh . . .' Angie followed, sighing as if her heart was broken.

'Ooohhh . . .' Gaby heaved mournfully. She took a sneaky look up at the sky and pointed gleefully at the three large grey clouds moving overhead.

'Ooooh . . .'

'Aahhh . . .' Twenty seconds later, the first drops of rain began to fall, and a minute later it was raining quite heavily.

✻ *When angels sigh, storm clouds gather. When things are especially boring in heaven, several angels might sigh at once and this can lead to quite bad storms.*

'Game abandoned! Everyone off the field!' Sister Teresa called, running past with her habit bunched up in her hand.

'Certainly, Sister!' Gaby and Angie said, smiling angelically.

That night Gaby was last into bed. Just before she slid under the sheets she thought she saw a movement in the wardrobe mirror at the bottom of her bed and, before she could stop herself, she'd turned and was looking straight into the eyes of the Archangel.

'I'm dreaming again,' she murmured.

'Thou dreamest not,' said the Archangel in a deep, solemn voice. 'This is real. I am here, in the mirror. I wish to talk to you both.'

'I know I'm fast asleep and dreaming,' said Gaby
firmly.

'You cannot stay! You must come back!'

'Absolutely fast asleep!' Gaby said
with determination, and she slid
under the sheets, screwed up
her eyes and positively refused
to open them again.

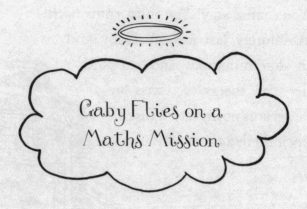

8

Gaby Flies on a Maths Mission

'Don't you ever take those vests off?' Marcy asked, as the angels rushed in and out of the bathroom the next morning. 'I reckon you even go in the shower with them on!'

Julia spoke quickly. 'Where they come from, it's the custom to wear vests all the time.'

'We've got bad coughs,' Gaby said, sneezing explosively.

'We feel the cold here,' put in Angie truthfully.

Marcy raised an eyebrow.

76

'It's the custom, they've both got bad coughs and they feel the cold,' Julia said firmly.

Marcy raised the other eyebrow. 'Oh yes?' she said. 'Sounds weird to me. Where do you come from, anyway?'

'I told you before – Nevaeh,' Julia said.

'Never heard of it!' Marcy said promptly. 'Geddit – never heard of it! Good, eh?'

Julia and the angels laughed obediently and Marcy, satisfied for the moment, went out of the dorm.

'Take no notice of her,' Julia said. 'She just likes to try and make trouble.'

'One of the angels was like that,' Angie said, 'always talking about you behind your wings.'

Gaby clapped her hands eagerly. 'What do we do this morning? What lessons have we got?'

'Don't look so pleased about lessons,' Julia said. 'It's Maths with Sister Gertrude.'

Seeing the angels' puzzled faces, she added, 'Maths is about numbers and quantities and stuff.'

'Is it a diddle?' Angie asked.

'A *doddle*,' Julia corrected. 'No it's not. In Sister Gertrude's classes we sometimes actually learn things. She's pretty strict, though.' She looked anxiously at the angels. 'I hope she won't pick on you.'

When Sister Gertrude entered the classroom, it was obvious to everyone that she wasn't in a good mood. And when she found out that she had two extra First Years, her mouth went even tighter and her eyes grew narrower.

'My classes are too large as it is!' she snapped. 'And I know nothing about you. Where did you go to school before? What classes have you attended?'

Angie cleared her throat. 'I've been to Halo –'

'We haven't had any formal schooling but we're quick learners,' Gaby interrupted, and remembered to add, 'and we're *very* interested in Maths.'

'We've heard that girls sometimes actually *learn* things in your classes,' Angie put in.

'Oh, have you?' Sister Gertrude said. 'Well, let me tell you that if you can't keep up, I won't have you in here. I expect a certain standard from my girls.'

She glared at them while Gaby and Angie sat, arms folded neatly, staring to the front and looking perfectly angelic. Gaby had discovered that you could get away with most things if you looked angelic, and Angie couldn't help looking like that anyway.

'Let's get on,' Sister Gertrude growled. 'The question I'm going to set you is quite difficult, but I expect you to provide a very good answer.'

The class groaned as Sister Gertrude spoke. They did it very quietly, though; Sister Gertrude didn't allow groans in her class.

'A very good answer,' Sister Gertrude repeated,

'from *most* of you, but from the two new girls, I must have an excellent and *precise* answer. In fact, if I don't get it, then their future Maths lessons will be spent scrubbing the school playground.'

Angie and Gaby exchanged looks.

'Now, this is an average

house brick,' Sister Gertrude said, holding one aloft, 'and the school tower is twenty-seven metres high. During this lesson I want you to work out exactly how many bricks high the tower is.'

'Can we go outside?' Sarah asked.

'Can we use calculators?' said Nicola.

'You may go outside, and you may use any means at your disposal,' Sister Gertrude said. 'Just come back with a result.'

Once outside, the class broke up into twos and threes and stood around waving their Maths books, agonising and muttering.

'I suppose the first thing we've got to do is measure a brick,' Julia said, chewing the end of her pen. 'We'll have to work out how many bricks to the metre, then multiply the answer by twenty-seven . . . or is it divide the answer?'

'Don't know,' Angie said vaguely. She'd picked up one of the school cats and was talking to it.

'Then again, some of the bricks are fatter than others,' Julia said.

Angie let the cat climb on to her shoulders.

'And have you frightened a mouse today?' she asked it, blissfully unaware of all the anguish and pen-chewing going on around her.

'Look,' Julia said, holding a ruler against a brick. 'All different. I can't see how we can possibly –'

'Four hundred and thirty-five,' Gaby said, suddenly reappearing at her side.

'What?'

'Four hundred and thirty-five,' Gaby repeated. 'That's the number of bricks high the tower is.'

Julia stared at her. 'How do you know that?'

'I went round to the other side, flew up and counted them.'

'But . . .'

'Sister Gertrude said we were to use any means at our disposal,' said Gaby. 'I just did as I was told. Come on, let's go in and tell her.'

'In a minute,' said Angie, still playing with the cat.

'I thought you were scared of those,' said Gaby.

'Not now; not any more. I like cats now. This one understands everything I say.'

Julia laughed. 'That's what everyone says about their pets.'

When they eventually went in, Sister Gertrude

was amazed and rather annoyed to discover that the two new girls had got the answer exactly right. She made up her mind to make Maths a little bit harder.

Someone else who was rather annoyed was Marcy. Having come up with the answer of one hundred and three herself, she couldn't understand how anyone (she) could be so wrong and anyone else (they) could be so right.

'I don't understand how you could have got it *exactly* right,' she said crossly. 'Not nearly, not almost, but exactly.'

'Just natural cleverness,' Julia said.

'The answer came to me in a flash,' said Gaby. 'A *flying* flash,' she added, and the three of them looked at each other and started giggling.

9

A Fire – and an Archangel

'The thing is,' Gaby said to Angie that evening, 'we must never be together in front of a big mirror.'

Angie put down her toothbrush (one of three that, luckily, Julia had been supplied with by her mum). She looked alarmed. 'You mean – the Archangel might try to snatch us back?'

'I shouldn't *think* so,' Gaby went on, trying to sound as if she really believed that, 'but it's best not to take chances.'

'If we get close to a mirror, might an arm come

out and pull us through, then?' Angie asked nervously, backing away from the small round mirror on the wall of the bathroom.

'I don't know,' Gaby said. 'But I should think we're all right in here. He could probably only get us through the big wardrobe mirrors.'

'B-but . . .' began Angie nervously. She stopped as Tiblet pushed open the bathroom door and began to wind himself around her legs, meowing furiously.

'Anyway, don't worry about it,' Gaby said. 'I expect he'll just try to talk to us a few times and then give up. We . . .'

'Sssh!' said Angie. She listened intently to the cat for a moment. 'Is it really?' she said to it. 'Are you sure?'

'Honestly!' Gaby said. 'You and those cats. You talk to

them as if they're human!'

Angie turned to Gaby in alarm. 'Tiblet's just told me that there's a fire in Matron's room!'

'A fire?' Gaby said. 'Don't be silly. How could a cat possibly tell you that?'

'You listen to him!' said Angie. 'Listen carefully. Don't just hear the noises, hear what the noises *mean*.' Angie tickled round Tiblet's ear. 'Could you repeat what you've just said, please, Tiblet?'

Tiblet obligingly started meowing while Gaby listened with a scornful expression. Suddenly, her jaw dropped and a look of astonishment crossed her face. 'I just made it out . . . he said the fire started from some wires going into a plug on the wall!'

'Told you!' Angie said.

'And Matron's still fast asleep and some books have caught alight and it's getting all smoky!' Gaby squealed.

Tiblet, bored with the whole thing, started to wash himself.

'A fire!' cried Angie. 'That's what they have in you-know-where, isn't it?'

Gaby nodded. 'They're supposed to be terrible and scary! Red hot flames and smoke that chokes you!'

'Oh, what shall we do? We'd better tell someone!'

'There's a little alarm bell thing in the hall — Julia told me about it,' Gaby said. 'One of us had better go and push it.' And she grabbed her dressing gown from the hook on the door.

'But how will we say we found out?'

'We'll worry about that when . . .' Gaby began, and then both angels started in fright as the small mirror above the wash basins suddenly gleamed like liquid silver, then began to grow in size. As they stood staring, the white-robed figure of the Archangel started to appear in it.

Angie clutched Gaby's arm and moved behind her. The figure of the Archangel grew more substantial. His halo gleamed, his vast wings shimmered with gold and silver hues.

'Angels!' came his stern voice. 'Hearken to me!'

'Oh, please!' Gaby babbled. 'We can't hearken just at the moment!'

'N-no,' Angie said timidly. 'Matron's room is on fire. We've got to go and rescue her.'

'Hold!' demanded the Archangel.

Gaby shook her head. 'Please,' she said, 'we really can't hold now!'

The Archangel waved his staff. 'You must not remain on earth!'

'But it's Matron!' Angie babbled. 'She's a big lady who likes chocolates and she's fallen asleep. If we don't rescue her then she'll die!'

'The wrath of an Archangel is a terrible thing . . .'

'Oh, please!' Gaby said. 'I'm sure an angel's duty would be to rescue someone from fire!'

'You are going against the natural order of things!'

'We'll have to talk about it some other time,'

Gaby said. 'We really can't stop now . . .' And without waiting to hear any more, she took Angie's hand and together they ran from the room.

They closed the bathroom door firmly behind them.

'Ooh,' Angie quivered, looking at Gaby in fright. 'We've really done it now!'

Angie and Gaby had been last in the bathroom that evening – the other girls had been in bed for a while and most of them had dozed off. Apart from Julia.

'You've been in there for ages,' she said. 'What have you been doing? I thought I could hear you –'

'Can't stop!' Angie said, tying up her dressing-gown. 'There's a fire! We've got to raise the alarm!'

'But how –'

'Get everyone up and out of the tower, can you?' said Gaby.

'And don't forget Tiblet!' shouted Angie over her shoulder.

The angels scrambled down one flight of stairs before Gaby said, 'This is taking too much time.

We'll have to fly!'

'Out of the window!' said Angie.

When they reached the next window, both angels climbed on to the sill, opened the catch, and launched themselves into the darkness. Their wings slithered out and opened immediately and they soared across the playground.

'I'll fly up, get in Matron's window and wake her,' Gaby called to Angie. 'You fly down into the hall and get the alarm bells going.'

Frightened, wondering what a fire was really like and what would happen if her wings got scorched, Gaby found Matron's room. The sash window was open at the bottom so she squeezed in without having to smash the glass.

Matron was deeply asleep in a chair, an open box of chocolates in her lap.

The curtains behind her were smouldering and small flames danced all along the skirting board of the room. Gaby stared, fascinated and terrified. She'd never seen fire before, but it looked so horrible and scary, flickering out of control, that she began to shake with fear. Hastily she tucked her wings inside her dressing gown and, pausing only to pop a coffee fudge into her mouth, began to wake up Matron.

Downstairs in the school hall, Angie had found the red alarm button. There was a notice by the side of it which said in very large letters:

DO NOT TOUCH – IT IS FORBIDDEN FOR GIRLS TO PUSH THIS ALARM.

She chewed her lip worriedly, then decided she'd just *have* to push it. After all, she thought, it didn't say *angels* couldn't push it.

Screwing up her courage and closing her eyes, she jabbed the alarm. All over the school, bells began to clang. Angie shuddered and put her hands over her ears . . .

Fifteen minutes later, two fire engines had arrived and a team of firemen were hosing water through the window of Matron's room.

In the playground, Gaby and Angie were lined up with the other First Years while teachers patrolled the lines of girls, counting numbers and double-checking that everyone was there.

'It's been so exciting!' Julia said. 'I'm never going to sleep tonight.'

'I still don't understand how they found out,' Marcy said.

'I told you – Angie heard one of the cats meowing,' said Julia, who by then had been told the whole story by the angels.

'But they're always meowing,' objected Marcy.

'It was a special meow,' Angie said.

'A very *loud* meow,' Gaby put in quickly, before Angie started telling everyone that they could understand animal language.

'I still don't see how a cat meowing loudly could make anyone think there was a fire,' Marcy said.

'You've heard of dogs raising the alarm, haven't you?' Julia said. 'Well, this was a cat raising it.'

'Seriously *weird*!' Marcy said, staring at the angels.

Sister Bertha, flapping her habit, arrived among the First Years all of a fluster.

'Now, girls, no need to panic!' she said in a high and terrified voice. 'The danger is past. You needn't be scared! Now, who were the brave girls who sounded the alarm?' she asked, and Julia pointed out Gaby and Angie.

'They heard the cat meowing,' she explained.

'Ah,' Sister Bertha said. 'The cat raised the alarm.' Her eyes rolled towards the sky. 'Heaven moves in mysterious ways.'

'Heaven?' Gaby angel-whispered to Angie. 'Been there, done that.'

'Got the nighties,' Angie giggled.

'Flapped the wings!'

Angie suddenly looked anxious. 'What about the Archangel, though, Gaby? What will happen now?'

Gaby was about to reply, but instead looked at Angie and gave a little scream. 'Your halo!'

'What about it?'

'It's coming back! It's because you've been good . . .'

Angie pointed above Gaby's head and clapped her hand to her mouth. 'You've got one coming too!'

'Quickly!' Gaby said. 'Before anyone notices. We'll have to do something naughty . . .'

Is there An Angel in Your School?

Here's a quick 'Angel spotter' guide. If you can answer *yes* to any of the questions, you score 2 points.

1. Has anyone ever come to school wearing a nightie?
2. Does anybody *regularly* talk to animals?
3. Are there people who say 'just flying off to see . . .'
4. Smell or what? Is there anyone who *never* washes behind their ears or . . . backs?

5. Have you ever seen anyone who can jump suspiciously high *and* stay up?

If your total score is between 6–10:

No way! You may well have a real-life angel at school! Invite them home to tea – now! (Don't forget to serve angel cake.)

If your total score is between 2–6:

Well, it's possible, or you may just have flighty (or smelly) friends. Try saying 'halo halo' to them (instead of 'hallo hallo') and see if they look shifty.

If your total score is between 0–2:

Sad to say, it looks pretty unlikely you've got angels at your school. Still, you could always pretend and look out for Mary Hooper's next TWO NAUGHTY ANGELS adventure, THE GHOUL AT SCHOOL!

Don't miss the next
Two Naughty Angels
adventure:

The Ghoul at School

Available now!

Turn the page for a taster of what's to come in
an excerpt from the opening chapter...

One of Your Wings Is Showing ...

It was evening and Gabrielle and Angela were in the small bathroom next to their dormitory in St Winifred's. The bell for bedtime had already rung and Angie (who always kept to the Heavenly Angels' Code of Conduct) had cleaned her teeth until they shone like pearls. She was about to go into the dorm and get into bed when Gaby stopped her.

'Hang on,' she said. 'One of your wings is showing. Here!' She tucked a few stray feathers under Angie's nightie and inside her vest. 'That's better.

We wouldn't want Marcy to see anything suspicious, would we?'

'No, we wouldn't,' Angie said, doing up the top button on her nightie. 'She's already watching us like a hook.'

'Not a hook – a *hawk*,' Gaby corrected. 'It's a bird.'

'Is that like a budgie?'

'Sort of,' Gaby said. She took a nervous look at the mirror. 'Don't let's hang around in here – the Archangel may be looking out for us.'✳

Angie and Gaby shared their dorm with five other First Year girls: Julia (their special friend), Sarah, Susie, Nicola and, unfortunately, Marcy.

When they were all in bed and the bell for Lights Out had sounded, Miss Bunce, their form mistress, put her head around the door. Miss Bunce was old, thin as a stick and usually draped in coloured scarves and shawls.

✳ When the angels are alone, the Archangel sometimes appears in a mirror to urge them to return to heaven.

'Now, girls,' she said, peering at them over her little round glasses and adjusting three scarves, 'I want you to go straight to sleep. We don't want any silliness tonight.'

Angie put her head out from under her duvet. 'Yes, we do!' she said. 'I like silliness! That's when we bounce about on the beds and have pillow fights and make a noise, isn't it?'

Gaby, in the next bed, stretched out her arm and poked at Angie to get her to shut up. 'Do be quiet!' she angel-whispered. 'You don't say things like that to a teacher!' ✲

'I'm just telling the truth,' Angie angel-whispered back, 'like I always do.'

'Well, I wish you wouldn't!'

'If you'd been to Halo Awareness Classes then *you'd* always want to tell the truth, too!' Angie said.

'You're not going on about those again!' said Gaby.

Fortunately, because Miss Bunce was slightly deaf, she hadn't heard what Angie had said about bed-bouncing. She went on: 'We don't want any silliness, girls, because tomorrow morning our dear Mother Superior arrives back in the convent and we must all be up early, bright-eyed and eager, to meet her. She's rather strict so it'll be excellent behaviour and best foot forward!'

✲ Angels can speak to each other in very low voices so that no one else can hear.

'Which is my best foot?' Angie asked. 'Mine both look the same.' She pulled up her duvet and stared down at her toes. 'Most bits of you are the same,  aren't they? Eyes and legs and hands and wi—'

'Where has Mother Superior been?' Gaby quickly interrupted. Since the beginning of term, Mother Superior, the head teacher of the school, had been away. The new First Years had never seen her; all they'd seen was her grim, unsmiling portrait hanging in the school hall.

'On an educational course,' Miss Bunce said. 'A special course concerning religion and how one can promote heavenly feelings.'

Both angels looked at each other.

'What are heavenly feelings exactly?' Gaby asked innocently.

'Oh – just to do with being nice to each other, I expect,' Miss Bunce said vaguely. 'No doubt we'll be hearing all about it. Now, straight to sleep!' she warned as she went out.

The minute she closed the door, Sarah sat up.

'Don't go to sleep, anyone,' she said importantly. 'My sister Hannah is coming along in a minute and she's got something exciting to tell us.'

The girls talked among themselves for a while but Hannah – a Fourth Year – was such a long time coming that Susie had fallen asleep by the time she arrived and had to be woken up.

'I couldn't get out before!' Hannah puffed, out of breath from having run up the eighty steps to the top of the tower where the First Years' dorm was. She plonked herself down on Sarah's bed. 'Sister Gerty has got wind that something's up. She was hanging around outside our dorm for ages, then luckily someone called her away and I just got out and flew straight up here.'

The younger girls looked at her with interest, wondering what it was she'd come to tell them. Only Angie was frowning.

'You didn't really fly,' she said, 'because you

can't. Only *angels* can fly.'

'That's just an expression,' Gaby said quickly, before Angie could drop them right in it. 'Anyway, lots of things can fly: birds and butterflies and moths and –'

'*Us!*' said Angie in an angel-whisper.

'Oh, do go on, Hannah!' Julia said. 'What's the big secret?'

To discover the 'big secret', read
The Ghoul at School,
the second in the
Two Naughty Angels series.